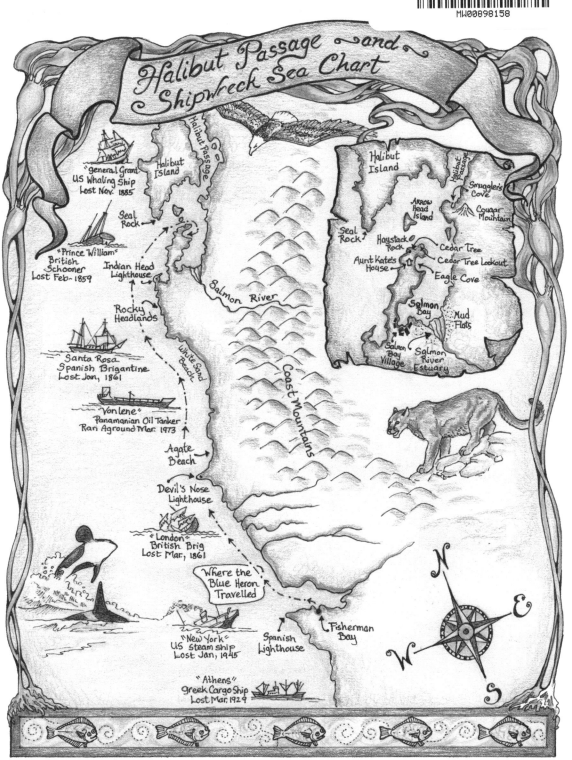

Halibut Passage and Shipwreck Sea Chart

"General Grant" US Whaling Ship Lost Nov. 1855

Halibut Island

Halibut Passage

Seal Rock

"Prince William" British Schooner Lost Feb. 1859

Indian Head Lighthouse

Rocky Headlands

Santa Rosa Spanish Brigantine Lost Jan. 1861

White Sand Beach

"Van Lene" Panamanian Oil Tanker Ran Aground Mar. 1973

Agate Beach

Salmon River

Coast Mountains

Devil's Nose Lighthouse

"London" British Brig Lost Mar. 1861

Where the Blue Heron Travelled

"New York" US steam ship Lost Jan. 1945

Spanish Lighthouse

Fisherman Bay

"Athens" Greek Cargo Ship Lost Mar. 1929

Halibut Island

Smuggler's Cove

Halibut Passage

Arrow Head Island

Cougar Mountain

Seal Rock

Haystack Rock

Cedar Tree

Aunt Kate's House

Cedar Tree Lookout

Eagle Cove

Salmon Bay

Mud Flats

Salmon Bay Village

Salmon River Estuary

N E W S

Lynne!

Inspirational teacher
& students of all ages.

Gina Snoely

NAME Conference
Port Townsend 2019

EXPLORE the ROCKY SHORE

with SAM and CRYSTAL

Gloria Snively

ILLUSTRATED BY Karen Gillmore

HERITAGE

VICTORIA · VANCOUVER · CALGARY

To my husband, John Corsiglia, for his wisdom and
constant kindness; my daughter, Alicia; my grandchildren,
Eulalie and Gryphon; and all children, whose love of nature has always
served as a source of inspiration. May the planet remain beautiful and rich
with its great diversity of species for all generations to come.

Heritage House Publishing Company Ltd.
heritagehouse.ca

CATALOGUING INFORMATION AVAILABLE FROM LIBRARY AND ARCHIVES CANADA

978-1-77203-236-9 (cloth)
978-1-77203-256-7 (pbk)
978-1-77203-238-3 (epdf)

Edited by Lara Kordic
Proofread by Lenore Hietkamp
Cover and interior book design by Jacqui Thomas
Cover and interior illustrations by Karen Gillmore

The interior of this book was produced on FSC®-certified, acid-free paper,
processed chlorine free, and printed with vegetable-based inks.

We acknowledge the financial support of the Government of Canada through the Canada Book
Fund (CBF) and the Canada Council for the Arts, and the Province of British Columbia through
the British Columbia Arts Council and the Book Publishing Tax Credit.

22 21 20 19 18 1 2 3 4 5

Printed in Canada

Acknowledgements

Gilakas'la. I wish to gratefully acknowledge the former Chief of the 'Namgis First Nation, Kwax̱alanukwa'me' 'N̲amugwis Bill Cranmer, and the 'N̲amgis Nation Council, 'Yalis (Alert Bay), home of the Killer Whale, for supporting my work over the past forty years. The Kwakwa̱ka̱'wakw people, the Salmon People, have lived and thrived on the central BC coast since time immemorial. A very special thank you to G̲a'ax̱sta̱las Flora Cook, principal of the Alert Bay School, for her support and guidance over the years, and also to the Kwak'wala language and culture teachers for sharing their considerable knowledge and wisdom: 'Ma̱m'xu'yugwa Auntie Ethel Alfred, Gwi'molas Vera Newman, Tła̱lila̱wikw Pauline Alfred, and Tidi Nelson. To 'Wadzidalaga Gloria Alfred, G̲wix̱sisa̱las Emily Aitkin, 'Nalaga Donna Cranmer (principal of Wagalus School, Fort Rupert), 'Wełila'ogwa Irene Isaac (district principal of North Vancouver Island), Klaapalasugwela/Maxwagila Nella Nelson (Aboriginal Nations Education, Victoria School District), Mupenkin John Lyall (vice-principal of Edward Miln Secodary School, Sooke), Musgam'dzi Kaleb Child (Aboriginal Education, BC Ministry of Education), I wish to express my deep appreciation for their friendship and support. What has brought us together is our common love of family, the ocean, the seashore, and all plants, animals, and entities of our blue planet.

Through the character of Aunt Kate, a retired marine biologist, the children in this book explore basic marine ecology concepts. Through the words of Ada and Grandfather Sculpin, the children experience a glimpse into an Indigenous view of knowledge and learning. The Elders teach that all plants and animals are connected and related. When we take care of nature, nature takes care of us. By becoming Tidepool Sculpins, Sam and Crystal learn all about their animal cousins and are encouraged to show respect and feel empathy with all of creation. It is my hope that the adventures of Sam and Crystal will help children embrace all plants and animals as family.

G̲ilakas'la.

An Unforgettable Fishing Trip

It was early in the morning when the *Blue Heron* left the protected waters of Eagle Cove and ploughed through the waves as it headed out to sea. Crystal and her little brother, Sam, stood on the deck and watched the sun come up. The children were happy looking at the blue sky and the bright yellow and deep burnt orange of the rising sun.

They couldn't imagine what the rest of the day would have in store for them. But one thing they did know was that none of the other kids at school were having as interesting a spring break as they were. Their aunt Kate, a retired marine biologist, and uncle Charlie, one of the best fishermen on the coast, were spending the week showing the kids all the creatures that swam, crawled, and flew in this remote part of the world. So far on their vacation they had seen White-sided Dolphins, Killer Whales, Harbour Seals, Bald Eagles, and a wide variety of critters that live in the Spray Zone and the High Tide Zone—two tidal zones that hadn't seemed that exciting at first, but once the children knew what to look for, they were pretty fascinating.

While Aunt Kate steered the seine boat in a northwest direction towards Seal Rock, Uncle Charlie showed the children how to set up the fishing pole to fish for salmon.

"Coho Salmon," he explained, "is one of the smaller salmon, just the right size for beginners."

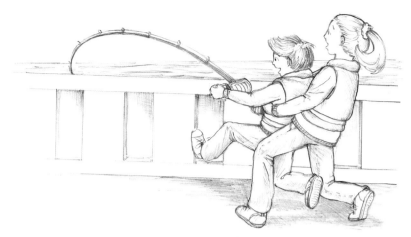

Inside his fishing box was enough frozen herring for bait, along with hooks, weights, and fishing line to make two fishing sets. Sam and Crystal watched Uncle Charlie attach a lead weight and a three-pronged hook to a line. To complete the set, he attached the bait to the hook and tested the line for strength.

"This is a good spot to fish for salmon," he announced. "I often see Harbour Seals and sea lions here, and sometimes I see a sea lion with a salmon in its mouth. This is how fishermen know where to fish for certain kinds of fish."

Aunt Kate killed the motor and allowed the seiner to drift.

"Okay, guys. Get your fishing rods ready to lower your line over the side of the boat. Watch me, and then you do what I do."

The children watched Uncle Charlie carefully. Then they lowered their lines over the side of the boat.

It wasn't long before Crystal yelled, "I feel something pulling hard on the line. Help!"

"Give a good hard tug to make sure you've hooked it," yelled Uncle Charlie. "Then start reeling it in."

Crystal pulled as hard as she could. Then she reeled and reeled. The salmon was strong, but she was determined to be stronger. It took five minutes for Crystal to bring the salmon to the surface. When the salmon's nose reached the surface of the water, Uncle Charlie used a large dip net to pull it out of the water. The fish flapped about on the deck until Uncle Charlie used a wooden club to kill the fish, and then it was over.

Crystal winced at the sight of the bloody Coho at her feet, but she didn't have time to feel bad about it before Sam started screaming, "I got a big fish. A *really* big fish!"

WHRRRRRR! The line on Sam's fishing rod went out fast! When the fish got to the end of the line, the force of it almost sent Sam flying overboard. But Sam was a fighter. He held tight to the fishing rod. The fishing rod bent down, down, down until it seemed that the rod would break into two pieces.

The feisty fish jumped, fell back into the water, and jumped again. It wasn't a small Coho Salmon. It was a huge Chinook or King Salmon, sometimes called a Spring or Tyee. The salmon weighed more than Sam, at least thirty-six kilograms (eighty pounds)! There was no way Sam could land the fish, and he knew it. Luckily, Uncle Charlie swooped in and grabbed the fishing pole. He pulled and pulled and slowly began to reel the fish in. But just when Uncle Charlie appeared to get the upper hand, the Chinook switched directions and moved from the starboard side of the boat, around the stern and the motor, to the other side of the boat. Uncle Charlie had to move fast to the other side while keeping the line from getting tangled in the boat's propeller. The children raced to the opposite side of the boat to keep clear of Uncle Charlie's fishing rod and line.

The battle between the Chinook and Uncle Charlie lasted for more than twenty minutes. At last the gigantic fish grew tired and began to swim slowly along the side of the boat.

"You kids take the pole!" Uncle Charlie yelled, almost out of breath. "Hold on tight while I net the fish."

But just as Uncle Charlie leaned over the rail to net the fish, a huge California Sea Lion shot out of the water and snatched the salmon from Uncle Charlie's dip net.

"I'll be jiggered," yelled Uncle Charlie. "Those blasted sea lions! There goes our prize fish!"

Sam and Crystal could hardly believe what had happened, but they were determined to catch another fish. They lowered their lines over the rail again and waited.

They waited and waited. Nothing happened. It seemed that when the sea lions appeared, the salmon disappeared.

"We might as well head back to Eagle Cove," said Aunt Kate. "It will be getting late by the time we get home."

The two children gathered up their fishing supplies and the only fish caught that day.

"It's a beautiful fish," said Crystal, feeling a little guilty for having caught it. The Coho was shiny and mostly silver in colour, with some reddish scales on its sides and a darker back.

"It's a beautiful salmon," said Uncle Charlie. "I can already taste it!"

Blue Heron
Is a Cunning Predator

Once the *Blue Heron* reached Eagle Cove, the water was perfectly calm. The offshore islands and several haystack rocks provided protection from the full fury of storms and high waves. Uncle Charlie cut the engine and steered the old boat alongside the wooden dock.

In the shadows of the dark rocks stood the seine boat's namesake—a Great Blue Heron, fishing for dinner with his long sharp yellow bill. The heron wore his summer coat of fancy feathers: blue-grey with long frilly feathers on his neck and a white head with black side stripes. Determined, he stood statue-like, gazing patiently into the shallow water that covered his long black feet. Then suddenly, in one great lightning strike, he viciously struck the water with his bill. The victim, a squirming Staghorn Sculpin, was caught by its tail fin in the heron's razor-sharp bill. The position of the sculpin posed a problem to the heron because the fish's sharp spines could pierce the heron's throat. Skillfully the heron flipped the sculpin in the air and spun it around to recapture it in such a way that the spines pointed harmlessly away. The sculpin slid headfirst down the heron's big throat, bony fins scraping the gullet and making the downward slide difficult. The heron emitted a hoarse guttural screeching sound. He held his ground for several more minutes until the passing boat sent small waves of seawater lapping at his feet. With a loud shriek of disgust he shook himself violently. Then, with wings outstretched like an airplane, he awkwardly flew away, croaking a deep harsh grumbling protest: **ARK, ARK!**

On the shore Ada was picking mussels from the rocks and putting them into a pail. Then she picked up the drum and sang a welcome song: "Heeya, Heeya, Heeya Hey!"

"Welcome home, my friends," she called cheerfully. "Did you have a successful fishing trip?"

Crystal proudly held up the Coho Salmon she'd caught. "This salmon sure put up a fight."

"You should see the size of the fish that got away," added Uncle Charlie.

"That's what all fishermen say," joked Ada.

"No, it's true," insisted Sam. "It was a gigantic Chinook, the king of all salmon."

"I'll believe it when I see it," said Ada, winking at Aunt Kate.

"It's actually a true story," chuckled Aunt Kate. "It nearly pulled Sam overboard."

"Still sounds a little fishy," said Ada. Then she added, "Of all the fish I love to eat, Coho is my favourite. Its orange flesh and delicate flavour is best for grilling."

"You should come over for dinner tomorrow and enjoy it with us," said Aunt Kate.

"I'd love to," replied Ada. "And if you like, I can show you kids how to roast the salmon the traditional way, over an open fire."

"Mmmmm..." said Sam. "Sounds delicious!"

Ada smiled. "I should get home before it gets dark, but I'll be back tomorrow to start the fire and roast the salmon. The Elders say, 'Never drop a salmon.' It's important to be respectful."

As Ada got into her aluminum boat and started the motor, Crystal picked up the slippery Coho Salmon, careful not to let it touch the ground, and began the long walk along the wooden dock to the house.

The Sun,
the Moon, and the Tides

The next morning, Crystal and Sam set out to meet Aunt Kate on the shore below Cedar Tree Lookout. Just as it had been for the previous few days, the tide was high on the shore. The children knew it wouldn't go any lower for the rest of their vacation, at least not during the daytime. Earlier, Aunt Kate had explained that every day over the next week the tide would be even higher on the shore. At this time of the year there were good low tides in the middle of the night, but that wasn't very helpful. This was disappointing. It meant that all the critters that lived lower on the shore, including the Giant Pacific Octopus, prickly Red Sea Urchins, Giant Green Sea Anemones and Sunflower Sea Stars, would remain hidden by the water.

"I wonder what Aunt Kate has in store for us today," said Crystal as they walked down to the shore. "We've already explored everything there is to see in the Spray Zone and High Tide Zone."

Sam was silent, but he couldn't hide the disappointment on his face. He badly wanted to see what critters lay deep beneath the surface. But how could he? It was too cold to go swimming, and they didn't have wetsuits or scuba gear.

"I get that the tide goes up and down twice each day. I can see that. But what causes the tides to go up and down? It's a mystery to me."

"Great question," chimed in Aunt Kate, who was already waiting for them. "The tides are caused by the gravitational pull of the sun and moon on the earth's oceans. The moon influences the tides the most.

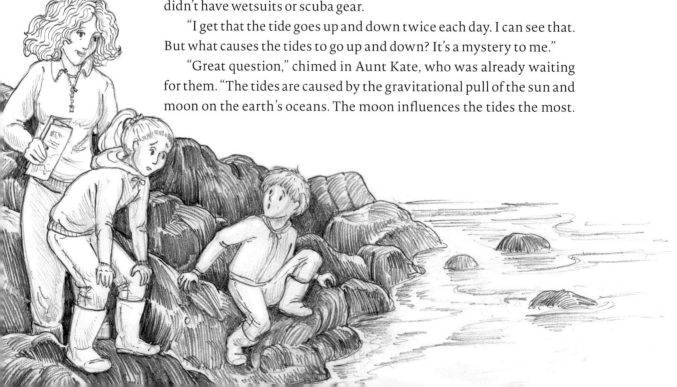

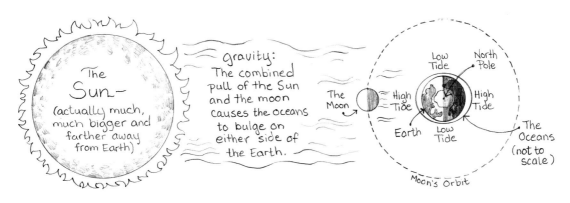

The Sun — (actually much, much bigger and farther away from Earth)

gravity: The combined pull of the Sun and the moon causes the oceans to bulge on either side of the Earth.

The Moon

High Tide

Low Tide

North Pole

High Tide

Earth

Low Tide

The Oceans (not to scale)

Moon's Orbit

The attractive force of gravitation pulls the water upward making the ocean bulge, which creates high tide in the areas of the earth facing the moon and also high tide on the opposite side of the earth."

"I still don't get it," said Sam. "Why would the water create a bulge on the opposite side of the earth?"

"That would be because of centrifugal force," said Aunt Kate. "It's like when you swing a bucket of water in an arc above your head. Centrifugal force holds the water in the bucket."

"I get that gravitation pulls the water towards the moon, but why are there two high tides and two low tides?" asked Crystal.

"While the earth is rotating on its axis, or spinning around," explained Aunt Kate, "two tides occur each day."

All this talk of gravitational pull and the earth rotating on its axis was making Sam's head spin.

"I wish I could become a sea creature and explore the ocean," said Sam suddenly. "Then I could see crabs and sea urchins and octopus up close."

"Imagine being able to swim like a fish!" laughed Crystal. "Sometimes I dream of being a shiny silvery fish swimming in the kelp forest."

"A lovely dream," said Aunt Kate.

Tidal Zone Organisms

[1] Black Lichens
[2] Periwinkles
[3] Small Acorn Barnacles
[4] Rock Louse
[5] Finger Limpets
[6] Purple Shore Crab
[7] Thatched Acorn Barnacles
[8] Sea Lettuce
[9] Black Chiton
[10] Rockweeds
[11] Hairy Hermit Crab
[12] Tidepool Sculpin
[13] Pink-tipped Sea Anemones
[14] Sea Sac
[15] California Blue Mussels
[16] Wrinkled Whelks with Egg Cases
[17] Purple or Ochre Sea Stars
[18] Black Chiton
[19] Keyhole Limpets
[20] Surf Grass

[21] Graceful Coral Seaweed
[22] Pink Encrusting Coral Seaweed
[23] Lined Chiton
[24] Red Rock Crab
[25] Goose Neck Barnacles
[26] Coon-striped Shrimp
[27] Sunflower Sea Star
[28] Green Sea Urchins
[29] Decorator Crab
[30] Red Sea Urchins
[31] Opalescent Nudibranch
[32] Giant Green Sea Anemones
[33] Red Encrusting Sponge
[34] Orange Sea Cucumber
[35] Plumose Sea Anemone
[36] Giant Red Sea Cucumber
[37] Bull Kelp
[38] Perennial Kelp
[39] Giant Pacific Octopus

Sub-tidal

spray
zone

high
tide
zone

middle tide
zone

Low
tide
zone

Tidepool Sculpins Are Colour-change Artists

Aunt Kate invited Sam and Crystal to sit down in the High Tide Zone overlooking a small tidal pool. She said in a soft voice, "Look closely. It's like its own little world."

Scattered among the dry rocks above the tidal pool were soft brown periwinkles closed up inside their shells, small brown crusty barnacles cemented to the rocks, and cone-shaped limpets clinging tight to rocks with their large muscular foot. They were all closed up inside their protective shell coverings, keeping the wetness in until the tide returned. The periwinkles and limpets glided slowly along, feeding on green algae. The feather-like legs of the barnacles flickered in and out, like a fisherman's net, to catch microscopic plankton in the salty water.

After a while larger animals ventured out from beneath the rocks and shadows of the pool. Purple Shore Crabs scuttled sideways from their hiding places before disappearing among the seaweed. Hairy Hermit Crabs went about their business of doing exactly what hermit crabs do, going from one empty snail shell to the next, trying each one on for size. The Black Chitons (ky-ton) were dressed in an armoured body made up of eight bony plates. Like the limpets, they had a flat muscular foot that allowed them to cling stubbornly to rocks. At the bottom of the pool, a crowd of shrimp-like amphipods, sometimes called "side-swimmers," busily darted here and there to feast on seaweed and decaying animals. Several Tidepool Sculpins—small fish not more than ten centimetres (four inches) long—glided gracefully from rock to rock. Once on the sandy bottom, they spread their fore-fins wide and appeared to walk.

Aunt Kate gave each of the children small nets and said, "Catch them if you can." While Crystal and Sam carefully trapped sculpins with their nets, Aunt Kate filled a clear plastic bag with seawater and put one sculpin in the bag. "Don't touch it, please," she said. "The seawater will keep the sculpin safe."

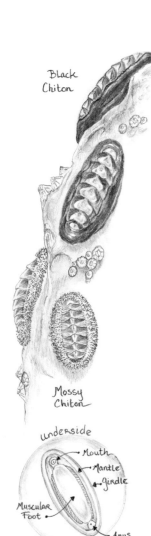

Black Chiton

Mossy Chiton

underside

Mouth
Mantle
Girdle
Muscular Foot
Anus

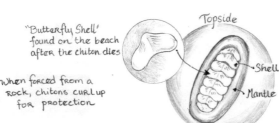

"Butterfly Shell" found on the beach after the chiton dies

when forced from a rock, chitons curl up for protection

Topside

Shell
Mantle

The sculpin sat on the bottom of the miniature bag aquarium, its mouth opening and closing, opening and closing.

Plastic Bag Filled with Seawater

"Hey!" laughed Sam. "I remember these little guys. They have such big heads for the size of their body. And they have little teeth too!"

"They're scavengers, right?" piped up Crystal. "I remember you talking about them the other day, Aunt Kate. We learned about scavengers in school. They're part of the clean-up crew at the seashore—the garbage collectors and recyclers."

"That's right," said Aunt Kate. "Tidepool Sculpins are scavengers like amphipods and crabs. They mostly eat dead and decaying seaweed and animals. But they also use their teeth and powerful jaws to crush small barnacles, dead crabs, and other animals with hard shells so they can reach the soft flesh inside."

"This is weird," said a puzzled Sam. "I'm sure this sculpin was darker when we first put it in the bag. It changed from dark grey to a combination of grey, white, and pink. How did it do that?"

"I know," said Crystal, remembering her school science class. "Lots of animals change their colours to blend into their surroundings. The camouflage hides them from predators."

"Right," said Aunt Kate. "Tidepool Sculpins can change their colours to blend with brown seaweeds, green Sea Lettuce, and even reddish-pink Coralline Seaweed. And the black, grey, or white blotches perfectly match the barnacles and shadows of the pool. I like to call them 'colour-change artists.' Speaking of predators, what animals might a sculpin be hiding from?"

"Seagulls and crows and maybe big fish," thought Crystal.

"Great Blue Herons for sure," added Sam, remembering the unlucky sculpin they'd seen the other day getting gulped down by the large bird.

"Actually," Aunt Kate explained, "a heron might prefer a larger meal. Tidepool Sclupins are pretty small, while other species, like the Staghorn Sculpin, are much bigger and live in deeper water. Of course, a heron will eat most any critter that moves."

"They'd have to move pretty fast to escape a heron," said Crystal, peering at the little fish in the plastic bag. "It's a good thing they're such good colour-change artists."

"The camouflage definitely helps," agreed Aunt Kate. "And there's something else fascinating

Tail Fin

Lateral Line

Dorsal Fin

Eye

Nostril

Teeth

Jaw

Anal Fin

Side Fin (Walking Fin)

about Tidepool Sculpins. One tidal pool is their home. When the seawater covers the shore, they swim to other areas of the shore to look for food, but they never travel deep into the ocean. They always return to the same tidal pool when the tide comes back in."

"That's really neat," said Crystal. She hadn't realized that a fish could have a home place and prefer its own tidal pool.

Suddenly a pair of black birds with pink legs and feet, golden eyes, and bright red bills landed in a nearby tidal pool and quickly went to work, prying limpets and chitons from the rocks with a quick flick of their long sharp bills.

"Wow! So cool," exclaimed Sam. "I've never seen birds that look like clowns before. What are they?"

"Those shorebirds are called Black Oystercatchers," explained Aunt Kate, "because they use their chisel-shaped bills to pry open small oysters and clams and eat the soft body parts inside. They also eat the muscular foot and body parts of limpets and chitons."

They sat on the rocks for a few minutes, admiring the oystercatchers' work.

"What are we doing for dinner?" asked Sam suddenly.

"Don't you remember?" asked Crystal. "Ada's going to teach us to roast the salmon I caught!"

"That's right," said Aunt Kate. "We'll have a picnic overlooking the sea. You'll love the way Ada roasts salmon, fish cheeks, and fish tails over an open fire."

"Fish cheeks and fish tails!" gasped Sam, making a face. He'd just gotten over the idea of eating seaweed. "Really?"

"Trust me. It's scrumptious!" said Aunt Kate. "We can roast potatoes and make bannock too!"

Crystal and Sam looked at each other skeptically, but said nothing. At home they often enjoyed barbecued salmon, and sometimes they went out for fish and chips, but eating fish cheeks and tails was a little too adventurous for their taste.

Aunt Kate shook her head and laughed at her niece and nephew. "You'll see. Once you give it a try you'll both be begging for seconds."

Small Acorn Barnacle

Common Acorn Barnacle

This barnacle can grow quite tall if crowded!

Area "cleared" of barnacles

Feather-like Legs, or Cirri

Black Chiton

Kelp

Tide-pool Sculpin

Kelp Flea

Rock-weed

Prayer to the Salmon

The short walk to Cedar Tree Lookout was through a beautiful forest of tall Red Cedar trees and Shore Pines. The path was lined with a variety of shrubs, ferns, berries, and wildflowers. The offshore view of haystack rocks was spectacular.

Uncle Charlie took Crystal and Sam to hunt for firewood. They had fun looking under fallen logs for pieces of dry bark and sticks of dry cedar or pine. Uncle Charlie used a small axe to split slivers of wood to make kindling. Then he showed the children how to make a fire using kindling and only one match.

When Ada arrived, Crystal and Sam watched in amazement as she used her sharp fish knife to expertly cut the head and tail off the salmon. Then she cut down the length of the belly and trimmed out the bones. She took two cedar roasting tongs from her backpack. Then she placed the fish's body firmly on a cedar wood frame and the head and tail firmly on a roasting stick, then stuck the sharp ends into the ground, leaning the flesh towards the crackling fire.

Aunt Kate took a package from her backpack that contained roasting potatoes. Sam smothered the potatoes with soft butter and wrapped them in tin foil. Then he carefully placed the potatoes on the coals burning low, near the edge of the fire. While Sam prepared the potatoes, Crystal helped Aunt Kate make Nootka Rose tea.

During their previous visit to Cedar Tree Lookout, Ada had showed the children how to mix dough and wrap it around sticks to make a type of bread called bannock. They had fun cooking the bannock over low coals, rotating the sticks to cook the bread.

When the salmon was roasted Ada removed the salmon from the cedar frame and cut it into meal-sized portions. Then she carved the fish cheeks from each side of the fish head and cut them into thin slices. She placed the salmon steaks on a wooden tray.

When the feast was ready to eat, Ada invited everyone to hold hands. Then she said in a very respectful voice:

Oh friends, the wild salmon, long life givers,
Thank you for giving your lives and bodies
to provide food for us,
Thank you for swimming the long, long
journey from the rivers to the ocean.
Thank you for finding your way back home.
O friends, long life givers.

Then she said, "Let the feast begin!"

The slow-roasted salmon had a smoky flavour that was delicious, and the baked potatoes and bannock tasted heavenly smothered in butter.

When Ada brought a plate with the tail and thin slices of fish cheeks to the table, Crystal and Sam said they were full and couldn't eat another bite.

"All the more for us," chuckled Uncle Charlie. "I love salmon cheeks and tails."

For a moment Sam was relieved that they seemed to be off the hook, but then Ada said, "It's important that we respect the salmon. The Elders say nothing should be wasted. If the salmon feels insulted, they will not return to our river. That is why my people eat every part of the salmon."

Not wanting to disrespect the salmon—or Ada—Crystal gingerly took a thin slice of salmon cheek from the tray and gave Sam a big-sister look, urging him to do the same.

"Okay," said Sam hesitantly. "I'll try a cheek."

As he took a tiny bite, his eyes widened in surprise. "Mmmmm! Its scrum-dili-icious!"

"Yᴜᴍ!" agreed Crystal after taking her first bite. "This is some of the best salmon I've ever tasted! I can hardly believe I'm eating part of a fish's face!"

Ada laughed. "I'm glad you two like it. I know it must be different from the way you cook salmon at home."

"Different and better," said Sam with his mouth full.

"Oh!" Aunt Kate exclaimed, suddenly remembering something. "Guess what I found this afternoon?"

Sam and Crystal stared at her blankly.

"I'll give you a hint," their aunt said. "It's something that will help us observe sea creatures that live in the Low Tide Zone."

"Seriously?!" said Crystal excitedly, just as Sam jumped out of his seat and shouted, "Scuba gear?!"

"Not scuba gear," Aunt Kate chuckled. "But almost as good. It's my old viewing box!"

She was met with more blank stares from her niece and nephew.

"It's a waterproof box with a glass window sealed into the bottom. We can lower the viewing box into tidal pools and see what creatures come into view. It's not perfect, but a viewing box can be a lot of fun."

"Oh!" said Crystal. "That sounds . . . interesting." Sam said nothing, still thinking about scuba diving.

"First thing tomorrow, let's meet at the tidepool where we saw the Tidepool Sculpins. I'll bring my field guides and viewing box from the house."

Suddenly Raven, the handsome and mysterious black bird of the wilderness, circled Grandmother Cedar Tree and landed on one of her branches.

"If you think you're going to get my bannock this time, you'd better think twice," warned Sam. The last time they'd eaten here, Raven had helped himself to Uncle Charlie's bannock.

Raven ignored Sam's scolding and seemed to talk to himself, mixing croaks, clicks, gurgles, and bill claps in entertaining ramblings: **CR-R-RUCK! CR-R-RUCK! TOK, TOK!**

Ada was silent for a long time. Then she said, "Maybe there is a reason that we are seeing Raven again today. As you know, my people have always respected Raven for his intelligence and playfulness. He is both a trickster and a teacher."

Crystal listened intently.

Sam was confused. "What do you mean?" he asked. "Is Raven here to teach us or to trick us?"

"Maybe a bit of both." Ada laughed. Then she turned to Aunt Kate and Uncle Charlie. "The children want to see seashore animals that live low on the shore, but the tide is not low enough to see them. Perhaps we could think about Grandfather Sculpin, the ancient one from the sea. He is wise and could teach the children about the animals that live in the Low Tide Zone because they are all cousins. Sometimes he takes people into his world."

"We saw Tidepool Sculpins today," cut in Sam, "but they didn't look like anyone's grandfather."

"Grandfather Sculpin is no ordinary sculpin," Ada told him. "He knows all about life at the seashore. All the seashore creatures are his cousins and they all live together. The Elders say, 'When we stay still and listen to the seashore, to the water, wind, and animals, they can teach us things.'"

Sam and Crystal didn't understand exactly what Ada meant, or who this mysterious Grandfather Sculpin was, or what he had to do with Raven showing up, but somehow they believed it would all become clear if they listened and watched the seashore carefully.

Grandfather Sculpin
Is Not an Ordinary Fish

The next morning, Sam and Crystal walked back to the tidepool where they had first observed the Tidepool Sculpins. They sat down beside the pool to wait for Aunt Kate. A few minutes later, Crystal glanced into the pool and nearly jumped out of her skin. A fish was staring straight up at her. This was no ordinary Tidepool Sculpin. For one thing, it was larger than the other sculpins. But more than that, this beautiful sculpin looked at Crystal and Sam with a sense of wisdom and understanding that is rarely seen in the eyes of a fish. Indeed, this sculpin seemed to know them somehow. He almost looked as though he had something to tell them.

But, wait. No. That was silly.

"Uh, Sam?" said Crystal cautiously. "Does this fish seem a bit . . . strange to you?"

Sam knelt down on the rock and leaned over the pool to get a closer look. The sculpin stared Sam straight in the eye. If he didn't know better, Sam could have sworn the fish was amused.

"Whoa," said Sam. "I think I see what you mean."

Crystal shook her head, as if to shake out the notion of a wise, all-knowing fish. "I wonder what's keeping Aunt Kate," she said. "Maybe we should've offered to help her carry the viewing box."

Sam said nothing. He and the fish were still staring at each other, eyeball to eyeball.

"Sam?" she said. "Do you want to go back up to the house with me? I'm going to see if Aunt Kate needs our help."

"Nah, I think I'll just stay here," said Sam.

"You should help your sister," said a voice.

This time, Sam nearly jumped out of his skin.

"What the—?! Crystal! Did you hear that? Was that you talking?"

"No," said the voice. "It was me."

Sam and Crystal looked at each other in astonishment,

and both lost their balance at the same time. Luckily Crystal was able to regain hers and caught Sam by the collar of his T-shirt just as he was about to fall into the tidepool. They both tumbled backwards onto the rock, holding onto each other for dear life.

Just as they were starting to regain their composure, the voice spoke up again.

"Sorry to startle you. But I've been wanting to introduce myself for the past two days. My name is Grandfather Sculpin."

Sam and Crystal could hardly believe their eyes and ears.

"I'm not an ordinary fish," Grandfather Sculpin continued, stating the obvious, "nor an ordinary grandfather, but an ancient sea creature. I have a sculpin's head, fins, and tail, but I also have a mind that can think like a fish and talk with people. I have two families. Most of the time I live in the sea with my sculpin brothers and sisters, but some of the time I live with my human brothers and sisters. I was given the name Grandfather Sculpin by my fish relatives, because I am the oldest and wisest of the sculpins. It has been said that I know more about the seaweeds and animals that live in the ocean than anyone else."

Sam gulped, then collected his courage to speak. "Our aunt knows a lot about sea creatures too. She used to be a marine biologist."

"Ah, yes," Grandfather Sculpin nodded. "Your aunt is a wise woman indeed. But there are some things even scientists don't know."

Although Sam and Crystal were human children, they wanted badly to be able to swim in the ocean, at least as far as a Tidepool Sculpin could swim. Grandfather Sculpin knew this.

"I will gladly tell you about my secret undersea world," Grandfather Sculpin continued, "but first you must try to feel free like the water is free. Just think. We must have water to make rainbows!"

Sam and Crystal looked at each other, unsure how to reply.

"Would you like to swim in the sea like me?" he prodded.

The children nodded.

"Good, then it's settled," said Grandfather Sculpin. "All you have to do is think about rainbows and repeat these secret words."

Crystal shrugged at Sam as if to say, "Why not?" and the two children tried hard to think about rainbows while Grandfather Sculpin whispered:

I am a quiet human, peaceful and free.

I'm joining a sculpin family—just watch me!

Fast and slow, swim and dive,

we can zoom and we can hide.

Grandfather Sculpin will take care of me,

and I will take care of the water,

Tidepool Sculpins, and all the

creatures that live in the sea.

Sam and Crystal looked down into the pool of water and repeated the secret words. The pool became a rainbow, then a mirror, and two figures slowly appeared. Each had a long body, a tail, big fins, and a big head and mouth.

"What the . . ." Sam stammered. "I'm a . . . I'm . . . A FISH?!"

"A Tidepool Sculpin, to be exact," Grandfather Sculpin replied calmly.

Sam Sculpin was grey, white, and black with speckles of green. He would blend perfectly with all the colours and shadows of the tidal pool. He knew all about camouflage. He was also the smallest of the three sculpins.

Crystal stared in wonder at her own reflection. Her body was the many colours of the rainbow, which would fade or become more brilliant as she moved past barnacles and multi-coloured seaweeds.

Sam and Crystal Sculpin could now swim with Grandfather Sculpin to explore the undersea garden and learn about its sea creatures! He would take care of them so that no harm would come their way, and in turn they would not hurt any of the creatures they encountered.

"Now children, what would you like to learn?" asked Grandfather Sculpin. Sam wanted to learn all about Sea Otters and sharks, and whales of course. Crystal wanted to know about sea stars and where to find empty snail shells.

"Well, here's the plan," said Grandfather Sculpin. "We will first swim through the Middle Tide Zone and then the Low Tide Zone. There are some wonderful secret places that I want you to see."

But first it was time for a swimming lesson. "Watch me," Grandfather said, and he spread his huge fins wide and gracefully swam in a circle. "Now spread your fins wide and glide. Give a little push. Now try moving, right, left, backwards, and in a full circle. Follow me and slowly glide to the bottom. Now, spread out your fore-fins and walk on the bottom."

Swimming was easy, but walking on the bottom required some getting used to, and so did breathing through gills. Whenever a current of fresh seawater swished over their gills, the blood passing through the gills took oxygen from the water. Crystal and Sam would always need oxygen. Being fish, they could take it from the seawater, and for a short time, could take it from the air if they were stranded out of seawater.

"I think we're ready," said Grandfather Sculpin. "Now I will take you on an incredible adventure and you will see things that only a sea creature can see."

A Rocking Rockweed Nursery

"Follow me," said Grandfather Sculpin, and the trio swam into a dark forest of bushy Rockweed seaweeds. The olive-green Rockweeds hung down from yellowing gas-filled air bladders, like golden balloons, floating at the surface, holding the seaweeds up. Gentle waves caused the Rockweeds to rock slowly, to and fro, to and fro. At low tide, when the tide went out, the Rockweeds lay flat across the rocks or hung down like curtains, keeping the wetness in. Grandfather Sculpin said that the constant wetness of this thick seaweed jungle provided a protected nursery for a great variety of eggs, babies, and juvenile seashore animals.

It took a while for the two young sculpins to get used to the darkness of the seaweed forest. Grandfather said they should spread their fins and sit on the rock bottom. "You never know what amazing sea creatures we will see if we only sit quietly."

As Sam and Crystal lay motionless on the rock bottom, their colours slowly changed, mostly to dark mottled grey—the perfect camouflage for a dark seaweed forest. All sorts of wiggling, slithering, crawling, swimming creatures came helter-skelter on fluttering fringes of legs, fins, muscular feet, tube feet, or no feet at all. Tiny baby hermit crabs, tiny juvenile crabs, tiny sea stars, snails, sea urchins, sea cucumbers, limpets, chitons, and worms. A whole world of miniature seashore creatures clung to the holdfasts, stems, and flattened fronds of the Rockweed plants, or swam in the shadows of the rocking seaweed cradle.

Many species of snails, limpets, chitons, and fishes had laid their eggs on the rocks or stems and fronds of the Rockweeds. Periwinkles laid their eggs in flat jelly-like egg cases. When the eggs hatched, the baby snails or larvae would be released into the sea to drift as part of the plankton.

Crystal was the first to see a handsome flattened animal with seven pairs of short legs of equal size clinging to the stems and fronds of the Rockweeds. The camouflaged Rockweed Isopods (*i-so-pods*) were olive green, exactly the same colour as the Rockweed seaweeds on which they dined. Those that left the Rockweeds to go for a swim performed wonderful loops and dives, like airplanes in an aviation show.

The Rockweed Isopod clings tightly to the fronds of Rockweed, and matches perfectly the olive-green seaweed it eats.

Purple Shore Crab molting

A slit opened across the crab's abdomen like a zipper.

The crab wiggled and kicked,

And backed out of its old shell

abandoned shell

Sam noticed one of the Purple Shore Crabs was acting strangely. The crab seemed overstuffed, and that seemed dangerous. Then a slit opened across its lower abdomen, as if the crab had burst its britches. As the crab wiggled and kicked, the slit widened, like a zipper. Slowly the crab backed out of its shell through the slit at the rear. The crab's new shell was larger, soft, and wrinkled. Amazingly, the crab blew itself up with water to increase its size. The old shell, or molt, lay motionless where the crab left it—like a cast-off set of armour complete with body, jointed legs, and eye sockets.

Grandfather explained that the crab is a crustacean (*krus-tay-shan*) and has a hard, tough outer shell to protect it from enemies. Because crustaceans such as crabs, shrimp, isopods, and barnacles have these hard crusty exo-skeletons, they must molt to grow larger.

"That's amazing," said Crystal. "But if the crab's new shell is soft, how will it protect itself?"

"Good question," said a pleased Grandfather. "For two or three days the crab will do little but hide among the seaweeds or under rocks while the new shell hardens enough to protect it from predators."

"So, what happens when the crab grows bigger? Will it molt again?" asked Sam.

Grandfather explained that baby crabs and juvenile crabs eat a lot and grow fast, so they molt as many as seven or eight times a year. Adult crabs four to five years old molt only two or three times a year. Even very old crabs occasionally do a spring-cleaning of old worn shells to which barnacles and other creatures have attached. Being too old to molt is dangerous, because an aging crab dragging around a heavy shell is easy prey.

Just when Crystal and Sam thought they had seen everything, Grandfather Sculpin became excited, "This couldn't be better! There in the shadows is one of my favourite sea creatures. Let me introduce you to the most amazing mother sea star."

The female Brooding Star, or Six-Rayed Star, holds her eggs with her tube feet. After several weeks they hatch into young sea stars.

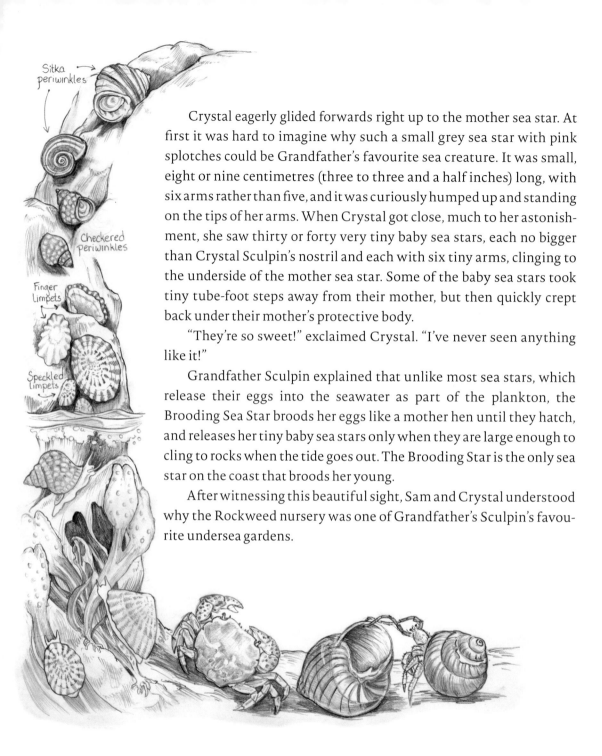

Sitka periwinkles

Checkered periwinkles

Finger Limpets

Speckled Limpets

Crystal eagerly glided forwards right up to the mother sea star. At first it was hard to imagine why such a small grey sea star with pink splotches could be Grandfather's favourite sea creature. It was small, eight or nine centimetres (three to three and a half inches) long, with six arms rather than five, and it was curiously humped up and standing on the tips of her arms. When Crystal got close, much to her astonishment, she saw thirty or forty very tiny baby sea stars, each no bigger than Crystal Sculpin's nostril and each with six tiny arms, clinging to the underside of the mother sea star. Some of the baby sea stars took tiny tube-foot steps away from their mother, but then quickly crept back under their mother's protective body.

"They're so sweet!" exclaimed Crystal. "I've never seen anything like it!"

Grandfather Sculpin explained that unlike most sea stars, which release their eggs into the seawater as part of the plankton, the Brooding Sea Star broods her eggs like a mother hen until they hatch, and releases her tiny baby sea stars only when they are large enough to cling to rocks when the tide goes out. The Brooding Star is the only sea star on the coast that broods her young.

After witnessing this beautiful sight, Sam and Crystal understood why the Rockweed nursery was one of Grandfather's Sculpin's favourite undersea gardens.

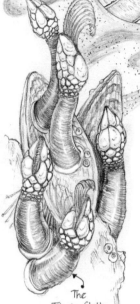

Muscle Attachment

Net-Like Legs

Mouth Parts

...the Barnacle casts its feathery plumes like a fisherman's net for plankton soup.

The Fleshy Stalk bends back and forth with the waves, like a rubber hose

Blue Mussel City

The three sculpins swam slowly downwards into a darker area of the seashore called the Middle Tide Zone. While Crystal and Grandfather stopped to admire a Mossy Chiton, Sam swam until he reached Blue Mussel City. The twin Blue Mussel shells towered above Sam. He tried to tunnel under the shells but was soon caught in a jungle of long thick byssus (*bi-sus*) threads that roped each mussel to a rock and one mussel to another. He started to move backwards but stopped in his tracks when the Blue Mussel in front of him suddenly spread its doors open slightly, like a book. Between the two shells Sam could see orange flesh that formed a sort of filter, like a kitchen strainer. The Blue Mussel began to strain tiny sea vegetables (diatoms) from the plankton.

Sam noticed thick colonies of strange creatures. The upper part of each large brown leathery stalk was covered with shell-like white plates of various sizes.

"What an odd-looking creature," he remarked.

Grandfather Sculpin explained that the Goose Neck Barnacle has adapted for living in an often-violent world where unpredictably strong currents and rushing waves beat the shore. "Its tough elastic stalk, or neck, bends back and forth with the surf. The Goose Neck Barnacle is a warning sign that this seashore can be unsafe."

Always curious, Sam Sculpin glided forwards and tried to peek into the nearest Blue Mussel, but the two shells clamped shut, almost catching Sam's snout. The mussel held its shells so tight that Sam couldn't get in. He swam up the side of the towering mussel to the very top, but he couldn't find a single opening. Just as he was losing interest in this unfriendly creature, a strange thing happened. The mussel's doors opened slightly, and a long slender tube-like "foot" stretched out until it reached the rock. The mussel used its foot, like a knife, to cut some of its anchor ropes, which caused the towering shells to tilt backwards. The foot moved forwards until it reached the rock a few millimetres away. Then a golden glue-like liquid, from a gland inside the mussel's body, ran down a groove in the foot until it reached the rock. A few minutes later, a golden plastic-like collection of rope (the byssus threads) hardened, and the mussel's towering shell-house was pulled back into

Byssus Threads

Grooved Foot

Sammy Sculpin watched as the mussel used its foot, like a knife, to cut some of its anchor ropes

The Wrinkled Whelk uses its file-like tongue and acid to drill a hole in the mussel shell...

Snail's Proboscis

mussel shell

...then inserts its straw-like proboscis to suck out the soft juices.

an upright position, but slightly ahead of its previous location. The foot had moved to a different location a few millimetres forward, cut one thread, and spun another soft thread that hardened into an anchor rope.

Sam Sculpin lost interest in the mussel's hard work and swam off looking for a new adventure. Thank goodness Grandfather Sculpin had not turned him into a slow-moving Blue Mussel! Being a fast-swimming Tidepool Sculpin had its advantages.

Most of the snails here were Wrinkled Whelks. Their frilly shells were variously coloured grey, brown, white, or orange. The whelks slowly moved over the mussels by advancing one part of their muscular foot and pulling the rest along after it in a sort of waddling motion. One of the larger brightly coloured whelks stopped moving right in front of Sam. He could see its long flattened muscular foot, sensory tentacles, and blue eyes. But he could not see the whelk feeding on the mussel. It used its file-like tongue, or radula, to drill a hole in the mussel's shell. The whelk drilled for about twenty minutes, then softened the thick shell of the mussel with a sticky acid from a gland on the underside of its foot. When the hole in the mussel's shell was large enough, the whelk put its proboscis (*pro-bos-cis*), like a drinking straw, through the hole and began sucking up the sweet juices and soft flesh inside.

When nothing more seemed to happen, Sam decided to move on. Had he stayed, he could have seen the whelk feed for twenty or thirty hours without stopping.

Sam caught up with Grandfather and Crystal, and the three sculpins swam single file in zigzag formation among the Rockweeds. Then Crystal noticed that the boulder in front of her was covered with thousands of clusters of yellow egg cases, each one the size of large rice grains.

"This is a wonderful discovery," said Grandfather Sculpin. "These are the egg cases of the Wrinkled Whelk."

"Gosh!" exclaimed Crystal. "Do you mean that baby snails are inside each egg case?"

Mussels have fine sieves which strain "sea vegetables" from the water

Thatched Acorn Barnacles

Adult Wrinkled Whelk

Called "Sea Oats," the egg cases are the shape and size of large oat grains

Each egg case contains 30 to 40 eggs

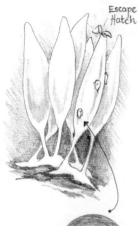

Escape Hatch

Baby Whelk

Day by day the eggs develop until each has a pair of eyes and a tiny, beating heart

"Yes," said Grandfather. "There are twenty-five to forty eggs in each egg case. There are millions and millions of tiny snail eggs on this very rock."

Crystal swam ahead to touch the nearest egg case with her fin. It was made of a tough leathery material that could protect the eggs from strong currents and keep the wetness in during low tides. Suddenly the top of one of the egg cases burst open, like a little door, and three teeny-tiny baby Wrinkled Whelks slowly crawled out, one by one, onto the egg case. After a few minutes, the three baby snails slowly crawled back into the egg case.

"Isn't that cute," said Crystal. "It's like a little house."

"Yes, the egg case is like a protective house until the baby snails get larger and they can find food themselves."

"What do they eat when they are such tiny babies?" asked Crystal.

"They eat the rest of the eggs in the egg case," said Grandfather.

"Yuck!" gasped Crystal. "That's gross!"

"This is the way of nature," said Grandfather. "Each egg case contains nurse eggs that provide food for the first baby snails that hatch out; otherwise none of them would survive."

The Storm

On the rocks just below the mussel beds, Sam and Crystal could see many kinds of brightly coloured sea stars: orange, purple, pink, red, and some multicoloured. Even now a bright Purple Sea Star with five powerful arms climbed the rock face in front of them, and glided on its tube feet ever so slowly up from the deep shadows. Crystal and Sam were amazed to watch its hundreds of tube feet, like bathroom plungers, pulling and shovelling its body along. They wondered what morsels of food a sea star eats. Soon the sea star reached Blue Mussel City and moved around carefully, feeling with its long sensory tube feet at the tip of each arm.

The sea star climbed up onto the largest Blue Mussel and straddled it. Three of its powerful arms fastened onto one of the mussel's shells with its tube feet, while the remaining two arms fastened their tube feet onto the other shell. The predator's pulling power was great, but the Blue Mussel had its own muscle power, and the two shells held tight, at least for now.

Meanwhile, another Purple Sea Star was winning its tug-of-war with a Blue Mussel, and the children watched the two shell-doors slowly open. The sea star slipped its own jelly-like, bag-shaped stomach from its mouth and into the mussel through a paper-thin opening between the shells. Then the sea star began digesting the soft body parts of the mussel right inside its own shell.

Grandfather Sculpin whispered, "The battle could take two or three days, but when the sea star is finished, little will be left of the mussel but two clean pearly shells to show that a sea star dined at this table."

The three sculpins hadn't noticed the sky had darkened. The ocean water was now full of movement. At the surface, the wind blew harder and harder. Small waves turned into bigger and bigger waves, until giant waves crashed on the shore as huge rollers tugged at anything loose. Rocks shifted and logs rolled, crushing millions of sea creatures. Time and again the three sculpins came near death.

Suddenly a huge wave carried the sculpins far up on the shore, into the Spray Zone, and slammed them onto the rocks. Noisy gulls picked and probed with their long sharp bills, and flapped and feasted all

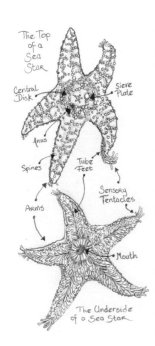

The Top of a Sea Star

Central Disk

Sieve Plate

Anus

Spines

Tube Feet

Sensory Tentacles

Arms

Mouth

The Underside of a Sea Star

around them. Nearby, a Great Blue Heron stood statue still, patiently waiting for any sign of movement. The three sculpins braced themselves. It was as if someone had yelled, "Look, boys! It's dinner time! Come and get it!"

With the hungry gulls charging from the front, and the cunning heron on watch duty, it was clearly time to hide. Sam was the first to slither under a rocky overhang, followed closely by Crystal and Grandfather. Luckily the overhang was too deep for those long sharp bills to reach them.

"Wow!" cried Crystal, out of breath. "That was a close call."

"We were lucky," whispered Grandfather Sculpin. "But we're still in danger."

The storm ended as suddenly as it came. The bright sun once again sent its red-hot rays down upon the seashore, drying every sea creature that could not easily trap water inside its shell or find a pool of water.

"There's not enough moisture here to keep us from drying out before the tide returns," said Grandfather very softly. "We're too high on the shore. We'll need to wait until the heron and gulls are gone and then crawl on our walking fins to the tidal pool below. There's just enough watery mud on the rocks to allow us to slither along. I'll go first. If the gulls don't get me, then you come too!"

The idea of Grandfather being eaten by a gull or heron sent shivers up Crystal's rainbow-coloured scales. The two young sculpins knew Grandfather was doing his best to take care of them.

First Grandfather rolled and covered himself in mud. Then, by moving very slowly on his powerful forward walking fins, he made the dangerous journey across the muddy rocks and submerged unnoticed into the tidal pool.

Sam and Crystal told each other to be brave and crawled one at a time on their walking fins across the muddy rocks before slipping into the dark shadows of the tidal pool.

When the tide returned, the trio began their journey back to the Middle Tide Zone. They swam past countless refugees returning

A Starfish lying upside down can use its many tube feet to turn over & walk away

If pinned down by moving rocks, a Sea Star can lose an arm...

...and Regenerate it back

As long as a single arm has a part of the central disk, it can regenerate four new arms~

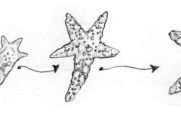

home. Those creatures still alive began feasting on those who were not, as is the way of the sea.

Sam was sad that so many sea creatures had died. Crystal worried about the Orange Sea Star. She had seen the rocks shift, pinning the sea star down.

Grandfather explained that sea stars have special ways of surviving in an often-violent world. "A sea star flipped upside down by currents or waves can right itself. If it gets pinned down by a shifting rock, it can crawl away and leave the trapped or crushed arm behind. It can even lose an arm and regenerate a new arm from the old stub."

"Unreal," said Sam. "Now I know why I sometimes see sea stars with one, two, or more arms missing."

Grandfather recalled his ancient ancestors—countless generations of Tidepool Sculpins who lived and died and laid their eggs under rocks in nearby tidal pools. This was the way of survival for all seashore creatures. This was the way of life in this dangerous yet astonishingly beautiful undersea garden.

Dangerous Sea Anemone Flowers

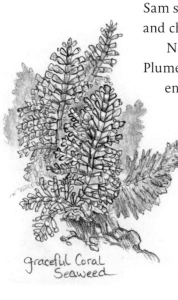

Plumose Anemones

Pink Coral Seaweed

Graceful Coral Seaweed

Grandfather Sculpin continued to lead Crystal and Sam downwards into even deeper water, into the Low Tide Zone. "This area is always covered with seawater except during the very lowest tides," he said. "This is a very crowded place, and it has few changes in temperature. Every rock and every cluster of seaweed is home to countless plants and animals. In fact, more seaweeds and more animals live here than in all the other tide zones combined."

As the sculpins slowly threaded their way lower and lower, Crystal and Sam were in for a wonderful surprise. The seaweeds here were amazing colours—red, brown, purple, green, and pink, and some every colour of the rainbow. Some seaweeds were the shape and texture of lace; others looked like feathers, ribbons, whips, fans, or water-filled sacs. Coralline Seaweeds covered some of the rocks, looking like splotches of hard reddish-pink paint. By far the largest seaweeds were the brown kelps that swayed to and fro in the distance. Their long stems and floating gas-filled bulbs acted like balloons to keep their stems and blades afloat. Each kelp plant had a huge root-like holdfast that anchored it to a rock.

The trio zigzagged back and forth among the seaweeds and canyons of the Low Tide Zone. Grandfather Sculpin continued, "You have probably noticed that many of the seaweeds and animals that live in the Middle Tide Zone are here too." On the rocky walls, Crystal and Sam saw familiar sea stars, mussels, barnacles, snails, crabs, limpets, and chitons. They also noticed many animals that were not familiar.

Not far below on a rock overhang was a garden of graceful White Plumed Sea Anemones, their long, white and sometimes golden stalks ending in what looked like a burst of white fluffy sea flowers. Grandfather explained that these beauties were not harmful to Tidepool Sculpins, but they were nevertheless meat eaters. They had feathery rings of tentacles that could capture tiny animal plankton from the ocean water.

Just below the towering White Plumed Sea Anemones were three Giant Green Sea Anemones. These anemones

Giant
Green
Sea
Anemone

were much larger than the Pink-tipped Anemones higher on the shore, but they looked innocent, with their tentacles swaying to and fro. Crystal was eager to swim close to get a better view.

"Hold on!" yelled Grandfather. "These sea anemones are not as harmless as they might appear. These imposters lure many sea creatures close and are not particular about what they eat!"

From a safe distance, the three sculpins watched as a Coon-striped Shrimp swam dangerously close. The shrimp seemed to be concentrating on its remarkable swimming ability—making wonderful loops and dives, like an acrobat in a circus. On one reckless dive, the shrimp brushed the grasping tentacles of one of the Giant Green Anemones. Instantly, the sea anemone began to close up, wanting to trap the shrimp with its tentacles, which were tipped with poisonous darts. At the exact second that one of the tentacles touched the shrimp's body, the shrimp gave a quick flip of its tail and darted off.

The shrimp was quick enough to race across the spread-out tentacles and catapult to safety, so Crystal thought she could venture near. She started to move forwards on her walking fins and saw a lovely Black Turban Snail creeping along a stand of kelp nearby. Just as Crystal reached the nearest sea anemone, a rollicking Red Rock Crab shot out from the nearby seaweeds and stumbled over a rock, knocking both the crab and the snail into the tentacles of the hungry sea anemone.

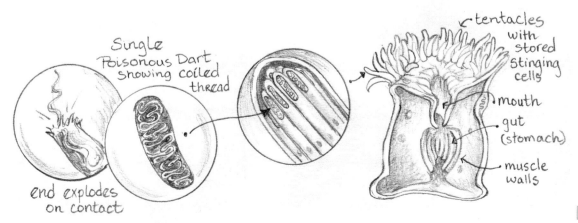

Single Poisonous Dart showing coiled thread

end explodes on contact

tentacles with stored stinging cells

mouth

gut (stomach)

muscle walls

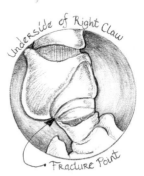

Red Rock Crab

The Rock Crab was large enough that the tentacles had trouble taking it down, and a tug-of-war followed. The crab used its powerful front pincher to pinch the sea anemone. Crystal could not believe what happened next. The crab detached its leg, and while the severed pincher continued to pinch the sea anemone, the crab easily slipped away.

Underside of Right Claw

· Fracture Point

Lost Legs Can be regenerated

But during the battle, the unfortunate Black Turban Snail bounced into the deadly spread-out tentacles of another sea anemone and could not escape. Flowery tentacles quickly folded over the doomed snail. The tentacles grabbed onto the snail's shell and folded over it, like a purse string pulled tight. The tentacles shot poisonous darts into the soft flesh of the snail, partially paralyzing it. Slowly, the sea anemone swallowed the snail whole, and in its closed position it was a sea flower no longer. Now it was a dark green bulge with a large lump at the centre where the snail had disappeared.

As Crystal watched, another sea anemone tossed out a shell , having digested the soft flesh inside. The empty shell landed in a graveyard of white broken shells—parts of snails, crabs, and sea urchins. Then the anemone slowly unfolded to resume its innocent-looking flower-like posture. Crystal was glad that Grandfather had cautioned her not to venture near the anemones.

Ostrich Plume Hydroid

• Hundreds of Hydroid Animals budding off in rows to form fern-like colonial clusters

Colonies of White Bryozoans covered the rocks

Feeding Tentacles

Individual Animals

Sea Plume Hydroid

Feeding Tentacles

Common Gut

Mouth

Bryozoans and Hydroids are colonial animals ...

... each individual animal traps food for the colony with tentacles tipped with stinging cells.

A Gorgeous Sea Slug

As Sam and Crystal sat on their forward walking fins in the Low Tide Zone amongst the forest of seaweeds, tiny sea creatures came crawling, floating, or swimming by. This ghost-like forest was thick with white, feather-like seaweeds that swayed gently in the current. Patches of white covered some of the rocks, like frost on a frozen winter window.

But things were not what they seemed to be. The white feather-like seaweeds were really colonies of tiny animals called hydroids. On closer inspection, Crystal saw tiny sea creatures looking like miniature sea anemones arranged along branches and stems—each animal budding out from its neighbour. But just like their sea anemone cousins, each trapped its own serving of plankton soup, using its tiny stinging tentacles tipped with poisonous darts.

The thin crusty patches of white covering some of the rocks and seaweeds were really bryozoans (*bry-o-zo-ans*). Each patch was actually a colony of several hundred tiny animals, each one living in a miniature box-like house. Like the hydroids, these colonial animals shared a common gut and dined on plankton.

Grandfather was the first to swim towards a luxurious garden of bright green Sea Lettuce. The trio was almost past the Sea Lettuce when the seaweeds began to shake crazily, and under it they could see the two brown eyestalks and long thin legs of a crab. To Sam and Crystal, a crab hiding in seaweed now seemed natural, but the garden of Sea Lettuce appeared to grow right out of the crab's body.

The fashionable Decorator Crab dressed in green was about to go for a walk, and she wanted a new dress to fit the occasion. Piece by piece, she pulled up some of the green Sea Lettuce from her body and tossed it aside like old rags. Then she carefully picked pieces of feathery white hydroids. She covered the tips of each hydroid with sticky glue from her mouth and used her long thin legs to carefully glue each piece to her back and legs. Her new dress complete, the fashionable lady made her next appearance in a beautiful white feathery wedding dress with a white Ostrich Plume veil decorating her head. She didn't care if the white hydroids would continue to eat plankton, just so their white feathery veils hid her crusty body and dangling legs from predators as she moved through the forest of white hydroids.

Grandfather Sculpin saw several nudibranchs (*noo-de-branks*), or sea slugs, on the seaweeds below. These snail relatives had no hard shells. There were many species of brightly coloured nudibranchs, and each species dressed differently—some in red, white, yellow, or grey, and others a mix of white and orange.

Sam and Crystal were astonished to see a gorgeous Opalescent Nudibranch slide past on a nearby kelp blade. A four-centimetre- (one-and-a-half-inch-) long ribbon of fancy red and white lace, it flowed and fluttered along. A clear blue line like a neon light decorated each side. This lady spent her energy growing clothes fit for a queen. But, with bright colours and no hard protective shell, she seemed defenseless.

"How can she protect herself from predators?" asked Crystal.

"As odd as it might seem," replied Grandfather, "nudibranchs have very few predators. Some blend so perfectly with their surroundings they are rarely seen. But even the more colourful ones are safe."

"But she looks so delicate. I'm afraid a big hungry fish would eat a nudibranch."

"The nudibranchs have a secret weapon to protect themselves," assured Grandfather. "Let's watch."

As the three sculpins watched, two Opalescent Nudibranchs slowly climbed up the base of a nearby Giant Green Sea Anemone. It seemed to take forever before the first nudibranch reached the top of the anemone.

"Now I know why nudibranchs are related to snails," yawned Sam. "They're soooo slow!"

Then a surprising thing happened. The nudibranch began eating the tentacles of the anemone.

"I can't believe it," gasped Crystal. "The anemone's tentacles are tipped with poison!"

Grandfather explained that some nudibranchs digest the tentacles of certain sea anemones. They then pass the stinging cells up into their cerata (spear-shaped outgrowths, or gills), where they are

For camouflage, the Decorator Crab dresses to fit the occasion—

She pulls pieces of green sea lettuce from her body...

...tosses them aside...

...then uses a sticky glue from her mouth to attach white lacey hydroids to her back and legs.

gills

Explodes on contact

Nudibranch Gills

Stored Poisonous Darts

Muscle Band

stored in special cells until they are required. If an animal attacks the nudibranch and nips off any of the cerata, the poisonous darts explode from their storage cells and cause the attacking animal to lose interest.

"What happens when another predator comes along?" asked Sam. "The nudibranch has lost its protection."

"After a few weeks the nudibranch will grow new finger-gills and replace the poisonous darts by eating more tentacles from sea anemones," explained Grandfather. "This helps explain why nudibranchs have very few predators. In fact, many nudibranchs sport bright colours and frilly shapes, as if to advertise their presence with an obvious warning sign."

"So," said Sam, "bright colours are like a big sign telling predators: 'No trespassing! Don't eat me! I taste bad and may be poisonous!'"

"You got it!" said Grandfather Sculpin.

"That's the way of the seashore. That's the way of the ancient ones," said all three in unison.

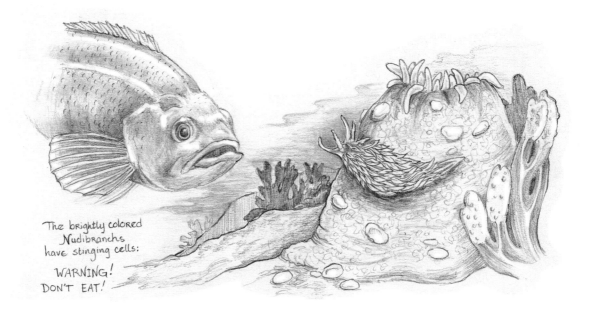

The brightly colored Nudibranchs have stinging cells:

WARNING! DON'T EAT!

Sunflower Sea Star,
the Terror of the Seashore

On the rocks, just below the forest of feathery white bryozoans, Grandfather noticed hundreds of holes the size of quarters in mixed sand and mud. Sam and Crystal were attracted to the chalk-white shells of several Cockle Clams sitting at the surface. Sam Sculpin was the first to reach the clams. The white shells towered high overhead. Sam swam up the side of the twin shells of the largest Cockle Clam, hoping to peak inside, but like the towering Blue Mussel, the clam slammed its shells tight. Sam didn't know that the soft clam animal inside was a mollusk, or that its two shells made it a bi-valve, or that clams and mussels were first cousins, and he didn't much care.

Suddenly the Cockle Clam sent out a short double hose to the surface. Sam could see a current of seawater flowing in one hose and out the other hose. Remembering the barnacles feeding on plankton soup, Sam asked, "Do clams feed on plankton soup too?"

"You're learning," said Grandfather. "Clams have a very fine strainer, like the mussels. They strain tiny sea vegetables (diatoms) from the plankton soup. Barnacles use a larger rake and strain larger plankton, such as animal plankton, from the plankton soup."

In the distance on a rock, an unusual limpet with a vent at the top slowly lumbered along on its wide muscular foot. Like its first cousins the snails, its one shell made it a uni-valve.

What caught their attention next was a long bizarre animal covered with warts that crept along on its tube feet, looking like a slow-moving, reddish-orange dill pickle. This Giant Red Sea Cucumber had five rows of tube feet running the length of its body and a ring of short, mop-like tentacles around the mouth at one end. Attracted by its red-

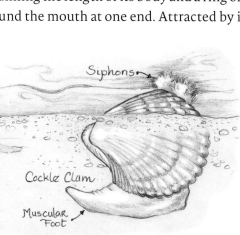

Siphons

Cockle Clam

Muscular Foot

dish-orange colours and strange appearance, Sam and Crystal started to glide forwards, but they stopped in their tracks when the animal began to stretch out. It stretched longer and thinner and stretched and stretched, and just when it seemed it could not become any thinner, it grew shorter and fatter again. Then it closed what appeared to be a mouth over its bushy tentacles, making it almost impossible to tell which end was which.

Sam and Crystal's eyes were attracted next to the size and beauty of a giant sea star as it gracefully glided into view. Its orange colour and twenty-four arms made it look like a sunburst.

"Wow!" cried Crystal. "Its colours are so bright it seems unreal."

"As a matter of fact," chuckled Grandfather Sculpin, "you might be interested to know that the Sunflower Star can be pink or orange or purple, and is possibly the largest sea star in the world."

"I've never seen a sea star with so many arms," admitted Sam Sculpin.

"Many sea stars have five arms, but the Sunflower Star starts out life with six, and over its lifetime it grows up to twenty-four arms. A full-grown Sunflower Star is so huge it can fill a garbage can lid and its legs would dangle a foot over the edge all the way around."

"Wow! That's gigantic!" gasped Sam.

"It's not only one of the largest sea stars," replied Grandfather, "but many of my cousins think it is the fastest sea star afoot. It can travel about three metres (ten feet) a minute! I should add that the Sunflower Star is a feared predator. My cousins call it the Terror of the Seashore!"

Sam and Crystal sat perfectly still, walking fins stretched out, bodies raised, eyes on full alert, watching. What unfortunate animals would satisfy the sea star's hunger today?

When the predator reached the collection of seashore creatures, fear gripped the neighbourhood. The Cockle Clams sitting at the surface instantly pulled in their siphons and extended their muscular

...to safety

...will send the clam springing away...

The scent of an approaching Sunflower Star...

47

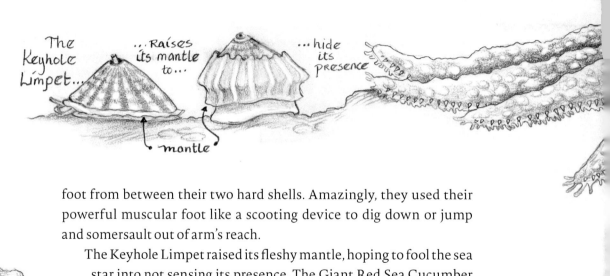

The Keyhole Limpet...
...Raises its mantle to...
...hide its presence
mantle

foot from between their two hard shells. Amazingly, they used their powerful muscular foot like a scooting device to dig down or jump and somersault out of arm's reach.

The Keyhole Limpet raised its fleshy mantle, hoping to fool the sea star into not sensing its presence. The Giant Red Sea Cucumber quickly arched its body up and away from the sea star's grasp. Several nearby hermit crabs picked up their borrowed snail shells and hurriedly ran away. The limpets and chitons clamped down tightly on the rock with their wide muscular foot.

"How did all those sea creatures know the Sunflower Star was approaching?" asked Crystal. "A clam doesn't have eyes."

"An excellent question," replied Grandfather. "Many seashore creatures, such as snails, limpets, and crabs, do have eyes. And those that don't have eyes can detect the scent of the sea star."

"Wow!" said Sam. "With so many hungry predators, I'm glad there are many warning signals to let sea creatures know it's time to escape."

"Yes," chuckled Grandfather. "It creates a kind of balance between predator and prey animals."

Mop-like feeding tentacles

mouth

anus

tube feet

Giant Red Sea Cucumber

The Orange Sea Cucumber

Feeding
Tentacles

Anus

The tube
feet attach
firmly
to rocks

~The Orange
Sea Cucumber
often lies hidden
among rocks and
crevices~

Bristling Sea Urchins

The three sculpins continued on their downward journey and found themselves in a beautiful forest of bright orange seaweeds. The orange trees were actually Orange Sea Cucumber animals, first cousins of the Giant Red Sea Cucumber. These sea cucumbers used their five rows of tube feet with suction cups to hold themselves between or beneath rocks. Curiously, where the five rows of tube feet met at the hind end, they formed a star. Crystal and Sam watched as the nearest sea cucumber used its sticky tree-like tentacles at the front end to trap microscopic plankton and decayed animal parts from the seawater. Then the animal put one tentacle at a time into its mouth and, in finger-licking fashion, licked them clean.

Sam Sculpin was attracted next to the gleam of white shells. These were the empty shells of dead sea urchins. The hollow balls decorated with a star pattern of bumps and holes were a clue to the location of their long sharp spines and tube feet when the animals were alive. Dead sea urchins had been tumbled and tossed by currents until their spines and tube feet had fallen off. Many small hungry sea creatures had feasted on their insides, leaving them empty.

The living Red Sea Urchins nearby looked like bright reddish balls that were somewhat flattened and covered with very long spear-like spines. Between the spines of the sea urchins were numerous tube feet that ended in suction cups, like those of the sea stars, only much longer. These sea porcupines were pulled along by their tube feet and aided by their long sharp spines.

Sam swam over hundreds of flat cookie-shaped Sand Dollars lying half-buried in the sand, or moving slowly along. The living Sand Dollars were covered with a thick carpet of short spines. Scattered among the living were dead white Sand Dollar shells. A star pattern similar to that of the sea stars, sea urchins, and sea cucumbers was carved into the shells.

Of the sea creatures Sam had met, only the fishes, birds, whales, seals, and sea lions—the vertebrates—hid their skeletons inside themselves. The others—the invertebrates, including snails, limpets, barnacles, chitons, crabs, mussels, sea stars, sea urchins, and Sand Dollars—grew hard shells to protect their bodies. Sam could see that sea stars, sea urchins, Sand Dollars, and sea cucumbers were first cousins. These echinoderms (*echi-no-derms*), these spiny-skinned animals, all shared a similar star-like pattern and ball-like body that could be shaped like a star, covered with long spines, stretched out long like a pickle, or pushed flat like a cookie.

The sea urchins seemed to like company, for they grouped together in large numbers at the base of kelp plants. At first, Sam was terrified that these prickly animals might attack, but the sea urchins slowly crept along and seemed content to graze on seaweeds. These sea creatures were kelp-eating vegetarians and were not interested in eating a fish. Sam could see the mouth on the underside of the nearest urchin, and around the mouth five large white chisel-like teeth came together to form a powerful scraper. As the sea urchin moved along, it left star-shaped tracks on the kelp where it had scraped and mushed up bits of it with its five sharp teeth.

Sam boldly swam into the sea urchin graveyard. He was not afraid. He swam inside a chalk-white shell, through the opening where the mouth had been. Without the tube feet and spines, the star-like pattern on the shell glistened in the sunlit ocean.

What happened next was a battle that Sam would never forget. Suddenly, from behind a seaweed-covered rock a huge Sunflower Sea Star with twenty-four arms moved quickly into view. Its thousands of tube feet worked together to enable the sea star to glide as if it didn't even touch the sea floor.

Sam Sculpin couldn't imagine how a sea star might win a battle with a Red Sea Urchin that was protected by those long sharp spears and a hard armoured suit. But inside the shell fortress was the soft and edible body of the urchin—one of the sea star's favourite foods.

Instantly, the sea urchins tried to escape, using their long tube feet and long sharp spines to move away. But the slow-moving sea urchins were no match for the swift Sunflower Star. The bristling sea urchin stood its ground and pointed its long sharp spines in the direction of the aggressor. This tactic had worked before against less dangerous sea

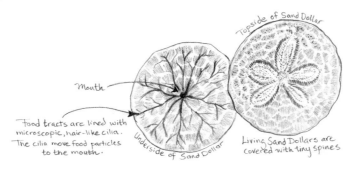

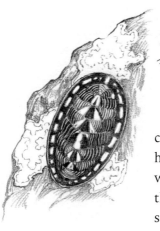

The Lined Chiton gets its pink color from dining on Pink Coralline Seaweed

creatures. But this giant predator was hungry and sea urchins made a hearty meal. The sea star used its powerful arms and tube feet armed with suction cups to hold the sea urchin down, then it humped up over the urchin with the tips of its arms touching the ground, crushing the sea urchin's long sharp spines. The sea star pulled and shoved until it crushed a crack in the sea urchin's shell. Then the sea star slipped its bag-shaped, jelly-like stomach inside the unfortunate sea urchin and digested the soft body parts right inside its own shell.

Sam was grateful that Grandfather Sculpin had taught him to swim rapidly, and he swam as fast as he could till he reached Grandfather and Crystal at the edge of the seaweed forest. While sea stars and sea urchins might be related, thought Sam to himself, they are not friendly first cousins.

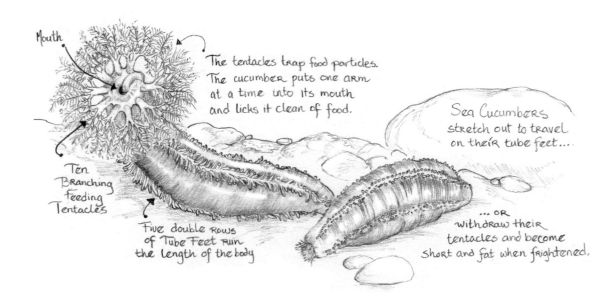

Mouth

The tentacles trap food particles. The cucumber puts one arm at a time into its mouth and licks it clean of food.

Ten Branching Feeding Tentacles

Five double rows of Tube Feet run the length of the body

Sea Cucumbers stretch out to travel on their tube feet...

... or withdraw their tentacles and become short and fat when frightened.

Lady Octopus's Sea Cave

Grandfather led the way to an undersea cave that cast deep shadows from within. Outside its entrance was a neat pile of empty shells: clams, scallops, and crab parts. What could have stacked the shells in such a neat pile? What was in the cave?

Grandfather suddenly froze. His eyes pointed to the boulder overhang above the cave. The young sculpins froze too. Perched above the entrance to the cave, a dark mysterious shape sat motionless and well camouflaged, as if guarding against attack. It was a Giant Pacific Octopus, the largest octopus in the world. The eight-armed mollusk had not seen them—yet.

Grandfather slowly crept backwards on his walking fins, followed by the two young sculpins. They edged into a dark crevice created by a nearby rock and pushed as far back as they could.

The creature had big yellow eyes and a soft boneless body. It had no ears, but its sight was keen, and inside that ugly head was a remarkably intelligent brain. The only hard part of its body was a parrot-like beak, which was surrounded by eight long arms lined with suction cups. Fortunately, the octopus had its eyes trained on something else.

Very slowly the octopus unrolled a long tentacle and stretched it towards a rock near the entrance to the sea cave. When the rock moved, Crystal knew it was a Dungeness Crab, the kind humans eat in seafood restaurants. Suddenly, with lightning speed, the octopus's long tentacle plucked the unsuspecting crab from its rock. The crab waved its pinchers menacingly, but it was no use. The doomed crab was swept up by the tentacle, and swept along by suction cups, as if on an elevator, towards the octopus's mouth, which was a hole in the centre of its underside. While the sculpins stared in horror, the octopus

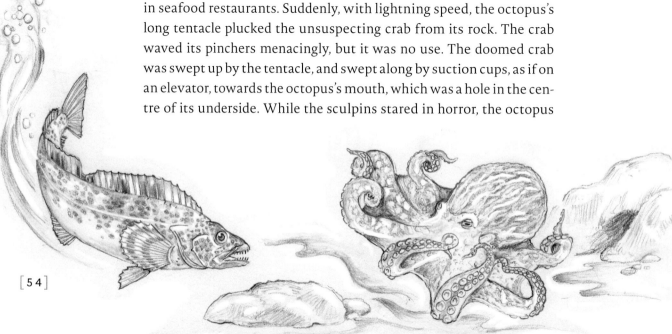

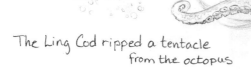

The Ling Cod ripped a tentacle
from the octopus

killed the crab by piercing it with its hard beak. Next it tore the crab's shell to shreds, and the legs and body pieces were swept into its mouth. Then, using a tentacle as a broom, the octopus dumped out its victim's leftover body parts and swept them neatly onto the pile of shells.

Just when it seemed as if the creatures in this undersea movie had calmed down, a large aggressive fish, a hungry Ling Cod, streaked through the water. Sharp jaws grabbed one of the octopus's tentacles. The Ling Cod did a barrel role, spinning rapidly around and around. Within seconds the big fish ripped a tentacle from the octopus. The terrified octopus changed colour, from whitish grey to red, puffed its body big, and spread its remaining arms out like an umbrella to scare the Ling Cod away. The fish was capable of ripping off every one of the octopus's eight tentacles, and the octopus knew it. The Ling Cod took a few minutes to dine on the tasty tentacle, then returned for a second helping. The octopus squirted black ink for a smoke screen, one of his tricks in times of trouble. While the Ling Cod attempted to find its position, the octopus made its escape. It sucked water into its mantle and fired it out through its siphon. That sent the animal backward like a missile, and its remaining arms trailed behind.

The black ink clouded the sculpins' eyesight and seemed to wreck their senses. The trio swam frantically in circles until Grandfather found a hole in the rock wall that he thought was the way back to shallow water.

"FOLLOW ME!" he yelled, and the three sculpins swam at full speed through the porthole into darkness. It was so dark that Grandfather realized the ink screen had caused them to panic and swim right into the sea cave. They had survived in one piece, but he knew they couldn't stay in the cave. They would wait until the Ling Cod and the octopus were far away and then make their escape.

But just as they decided to swim to freedom, a long suction-cup-covered tentacle blocked the entrance to the cave. They were trapped! Way back in the dark depth of the cave was a second octopus. Hundreds and hundreds of long ropes of tear-shaped egg cases hung down from the ceiling of the cave, creating a sort of walled nursery.

The female octopus lays up to 50,000 tiny eggs in long, sticky strands

She attaches the egg strands to the roof of her den

"This sea cave must be a mother octopus's nursery," whispered Grandfather, trying to sound braver than he really felt.

Fortunately, the lady of the house did not seem interested in attacking the sculpins but went about the business of tending her eggs. She rubbed her arms carefully over the eggs to keep them clean. Crystal knew the lady had seen the three sculpins, for she had looked right at them. Was she playing with them, just waiting for the right moment to have a tender morsel of food?

When Grandfather was sure the lady wasn't watching, he yelled, "Swim for your lives!" and the sculpins swam at full speed until they reached the shadows of the kelp forest. Sam and Crystal were puzzled that the Dark Lady had not attacked. Surely she could have taken them easily.

"Fortunately for us, a female octopus guards her eggs against predators like crabs, big fish, and even from male octopuses," explained Grandfather Sculpin. "That is why she barricaded herself inside the cave by building a wall of rocks nearly to the ceiling. She is a perfect mother. She hardly eats anything while tending her eggs and becomes very thin. Then, not long after all the young have hatched out and become part of the plankton, the tired and worn lady dies."

"Goodness," said Crystal, "I'm glad I'm not an octopus."

"Or a Ling Cod," added Sam.

"Ah, yes," chuckled Grandfather. "A Tidepool Sculpin is the perfect fish!"

Six months later, the babies hatch and are immediately able to swim

The Kelp Forest

Sea urchins leave star-shaped tracks—a clue to their **five** sharp teeth

blades

floats

stipe

Perennial Kelp
Sea urchins may scrape at the stems and holdfasts of kelps until the entire 12 meter long plant releases and washes out to sea or becomes stranded on the shore

holdfast

The three sculpins swam for a long time to an offshore forest of giant brown kelp. Peering down, the kelp plants looked like giant trees towering thirty metres (about a hundred feet) or more above the seafloor. Below the surface, long beams of golden sunlight streamed through the amber-coloured fronds, lighting a forest community filled with life. Among the kelp, Crystal and Sam admired schools of their larger fish relatives: herring, salmon, and perch swimming through the sunbeams in search of lunch.

The trio zigzagged down, down, down through the kelp forest until they found themselves on the rocky bottom where they were surrounded by dark shadows. Crystal and Sam noticed many species of brown plant-like kelp, anchored to the rocky bottom by their surprisingly large holdfasts, similar to the way tree roots anchor trees to the ground. Among the rocks and tangle of kelp holdfasts were the homes of countless animals, including snails, limpets, barnacles, chitons, sea stars, crabs, sea cucumbers, sea anemones, sea urchins, and worms.

"The kelp are not trees," explained Grandfather. "They are seaweeds, also called algae, and their holdfast, stipes, floats, and blades are very different from the roots, trunk, and leaves of a tree. But like a tree, the kelp plant depends on sunlight to make food in order to grow."

The sculpins perched together on a rock, sitting on their large forward walking fins, viewing the forest floor. In full view, an army of hungry Red Sea Urchins invaded the stand of kelp forest. The urchins chewed and chewed with their chisel-like teeth at the holdfast of a nearby kelp until they chewed clear through it, causing the kelp to float away.

In the distance, a perky Sea Otter hunted among the rocks for food. The otter picked up a rock from the ocean floor and used it to pry loose a Red Sea Urchin—one of its favourite meals. Then it swam with the urchin and the rock to the surface, rolled onto its back, and anchored a leg around some kelp. To Sam and Crystal's amazement, it used its flat chest as a lunch table. The otter cracked the urchin shell by hitting it with the rock. It used its paws to pry open the sea urchin, carefully avoiding the urchin's long sharp spines to get at the sweet meat inside.

Nearby a mother Sea Otter floated on her back with a newborn pup resting on her chest. The newborn looked like a floppy rag doll when the mother held it high above the water to lick and groom its fluffy fur. Of all the sea creatures Grandfather knew about, only the young of mammals—the otters, seals, sea lions, and whales—nursed on fat-rich milk from their mothers.

A sudden snort startled the Sea Otters. Then a pair of large black eyes peered out of the water.

"A Harbour Seal," cautioned Grandfather Sculpin. The seal snorted in playfulness, then spread its webbed feet, kicked, and zoomed off like a torpedo.

A gigantic Sea Nettle Jellyfish drifted in the current. Crystal and Sam did not know that the jellyfish is not a fish, but a jelly-like animal related to sea anemones and hydroids. The jellyfish had a see-through body surrounded by a ring of long tentacles armed with poisonous darts that could paralyze its prey. This cnidaria (ni-dare-ia), an animal with stinging cells, was not an innocent blob of jelly. Instinctively, Crystal and Sam knew not to get too close to such a large jellyfish. A small fish could easily become tangled in the tentacles. Crystal and Sam were learning to be fish.

A few minutes later, Grandfather Sculpin whispered in a low voice, "We are nearing the end of our journey. We cannot venture farther into the kelp forest because it is not our home. We must travel back to our home in the tidepool higher on the shore. This is the way of Tidepool Sculpins. This is the way of the ancient ones. But before we return to our tidal pool home, you can linger a little while and watch your animal cousins here in the kelp forest."

Sam and Crystal Sculpin were sad that their adventure was coming to an end, but instinct told them that they should find their way back home to the High Tide Zone. They took a long final look at the beautiful undersea garden. Then slowly they turned around to follow Grandfather Sculpin back home.

But to their great surprise, Grandfather Sculpin had disappeared. Instead they were back on the shore, sitting on rocks above the tidal pool. Aunt Kate came huffing and puffing, all out of breath, with her plastic bucket and plastic bag aquariums. She had walked as fast as she could to her science lab to gather up her equipment.

Bull Kelp

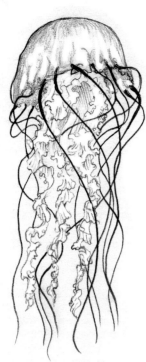

Sea Nettle
Jellyfish

"Here," she said enthusiastically. "I found my old viewing box in Uncle Charlie's workshop. We can put it into a tidal pool and see at least some seashore creatures lower on the shore."

"Oh, we already know all about the Low Tide Zone," blurted Sam without thinking, "and even the offshore kelp forest. We saw Purple Sea Urchins, Giant Red Sea Cucumbers, Rockweed nurseries, the Sunflower Sea Star, the Sea Nettle Jellyfish, and even newborn Sea Otter pups!"

He went on to tell his astonished aunt about why Goose Neck Barnacles act as a warning of an unsafe surf-swept seashore, why nudibranchs are safe from predators even though they sport bright colours, and why a mother octopus won't eat while she tends her eggs.

"Hold on," said a flabbergasted Aunt Kate. "How did you learn so much? I've only been away for twenty minutes!"

Crystal and Sam looked at each other. Should they tell Aunt Kate about their adventure with Grandfather Sculpin? Would she believe them?

Aunt Kate became silent as the realization hit her. After a very long time, she whispered, "Ada was right! You met Grandfather Sculpin, didn't you?"

Relieved, the children both started talking at once. They told Aunt Kate all about seeing the ancient fish in the tidepool and their magical transformation into sculpins.

Aunt Kate nodded her head in amazement. "Ada told me about Grandfather Sculpin, but I always thought it was just a story. I've spent a lifetime exploring seashores and studying countless seashore creatures and never met him myself. But I've seen enough amazing things to know that the seashore is indeed magical!"

That night Crystal and Sam made a visit to Cedar Tree Lookout. The half moon shone bright over Eagle Cove, and the stars sparkled. In another week a full moon would brighten the night sky, and its greater gravitational pull on the earth would cause the tide to go out low enough to explore the Low Tide Zone.

Crystal and Sam sat quietly for a long time, listening to the waves gently lapping at the shore.

Sam broke the silence. "Do you think we will see Grandfather Sculpin again?"

Crystal didn't know, but one thing was for sure. The two children loved the water, the ocean, and Grandfather Sculpin. The wise old fish had kept his word. He looked after them because they promised to take care of the water, Tidepool Sculpins, and all the creatures that live in the ocean. Crystal and Sam promised to take care of Grandfather's undersea garden because this was the home of their bothers and sisters, mothers and fathers, grandmothers and grandfathers. Grandfather had said, "We are all part of the circle of life."

The two children were not quite sure what future dangers might harm their animal relatives in the ocean, or how they might take care of them. But lovingly, Ada had promised, "When we stay still and listen to the seashore, the water, wind, and animals, they can teach us things." Ada said to search inside ourselves to find the true path to respect and harmony. She promised that if we listened to our animal relatives, the questions and answers would be inside themselves. This was the way of the ancient ones. This was the way it had always been. The two children held hands and vowed to keep their promise.

Eagle Cove List of Organisms

Look for the plants and animals of Halibut Passage and Eagle Cove on or near many rocky seashores throughout the Pacific Northwest.

BIRDS
(warm blooded, egg laying)
Bald Eagle
Black Oystercatcher
Blue Heron
Glaucous-winged Gull
Raven

MAMMALS (warm blooded, nourish young with milk)
California Sea Lion
Harbour Seal
Sea Otter

FISHES
(cold blooded, gills and fins)
Coho Salmon
Ling Cod
Staghorn Sculpin
Tidepool Sculpin

ARTHROPODS (jointed legs)
Amphipod
Common Acorn Barnacle
Coon-striped Shrimp
Decorator Crab
Goose Neck Barnacle
Hairy Hermit Crab
Kelp Flea
Purple Shore Crab
Red Rock Crab
Rockweed Isopod
Small Acorn Barnacle
Thatched Barnacle

ECHINODERMS
(spiny skins, star pattern)
Brooding Sea Star
Giant Sea Cucumber
Orange Sea Cucumber
Purple or Orange Sea Star
Red Sea Urchin
Sand Dollar
Sunflower Sea Star

MOLLUSKS (muscular foot)
Black Chiton
California Blue Mussel
Checkered Periwinkle
Cockle Clam
Giant Pacific Octopus
Keyhole Limpet
Lined Chiton
Mossy Chiton
Opalescent Nudibranch
Sitka Periwinkle
Speckled Limpet
Wrinkled Whelk

CNIDARIA (stinging cells)
Giant Green Sea Anemone
Ostrich Plumed Hydroid
Plumose Sea Anemone
Sea Nettle Jellyfish
Sea Plume Hydroid

SEAWEEDS
Bull Kelp
Coralline Seaweed
Graceful Coral Seaweed
Perennial Kelp
Rockweed
Sea Lettuce
Sea Sac
Surf Grass